My Forest is Green

To my daughter, Madeline, for joining me on forest
adventures, and my wife, Jen, for all her support — D.L.

To Kevin — A.B.

Text © 2019 Darren Lebeuf
Illustrations © 2019 Ashley Barron

Kids Can Press gratefully acknowledges the financial support of the Government of
Ontario, through the Ontario Media Development Corporation; the Ontario Arts
Council; the Canada Council for the Arts; and the Government of Canada for our
publishing activity.

Published in Canada and the U.S. by Kids Can Press Ltd.
25 Dockside Drive, Toronto, ON M5A 0B5

Kids Can Press is a Corus Entertainment Inc. company

www.kidscanpress.com

The artwork in this book was rendered in cut-paper collage, watercolor, acrylic
and pencil crayon, with some digital assembly.
The text is set in Cambria.

Edited by Jennifer Stokes
Designed by Julia Naimska

Printed and bound in Malaysia, in 10/2018 by Tien Wah Press (Pte.) Ltd.

CM 19 0 9 8 7 6 5 4 3 2 1

Library and Archives Canada Cataloguing in Publication

Lebeuf, Darren, 1981–, author

    My forest is green / Darren Lebeuf ; illustrated by Ashley Barron.

ISBN 978-1-77138-930-3 (hardcover)

    1. Forests in art — Juvenile literature. 2. Nature in art — Juvenile
literature. 3. Nature (Aesthetics) — Juvenile literature. 4. Forest ecology —
Juvenile literature. 5. Handicraft for children — Juvenile literature.
I. Barron, Ashley, illustrator II. Title.

N7680.L43 2019   j704.9'43   C2018-902056-3

My Forest is Green

Written by **Darren Lebeuf**

Illustrated by **Ashley Barron**

Kids Can Press

This is my forest.

Well, actually ...
this is my forest.

My forest is tall.

My forest is short.

My forest is fluffy.

My forest is prickly.

My forest is rough.

My forest is smooth.

My forest is wide

and narrow

and heavy

and light.

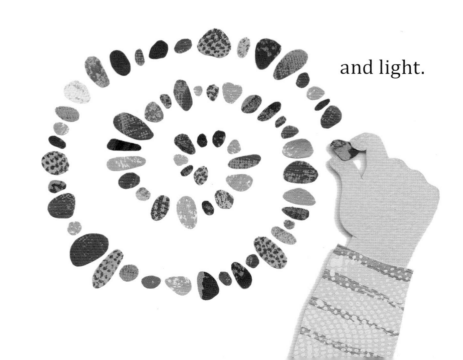

and small

My forest is big

and dense

and sparse.

My forest is crispy ...

and soft.

Sometimes my forest is snowy.

Sometimes my
forest is wet.

My forest is scattered and soggy,
and spotted and foggy.

My forest is green.
Twisty green,
shiny green,
jagged green
and wavy green.

But my forest is also dangling yellow,

tiptoe gray,

peekaboo purple,

sneaky blue,

patient white

and carefree red.

But mostly it's green.

My forest sings and dances.

Sometimes my forest is loud,

and sometimes my forest is quiet.

My forest is so many
things ...

I can't wait to see what my
forest is tomorrow.